D1540642

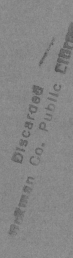

Marcy Hooper and the Greatest Treasure in the World

Marcy Hooper and the Greatest Treasure in the World

STEPHANIE S. TOLAN

ILLUSTRATIONS BY
KAREN MILONE

MORROW JUNIOR BOOKS
NEW YORK

Book design by Karen Palinko

Inquiries should be addressed to William Morrow and Company, Inc.,
1350 Avenue of the Americas,
New York, N.Y. 10019.
Printed in the United States of America.
1   2   3   4   5   6   7   8   9   10
Library of Congress Cataloging-in-Publication Data
Tolan, Stephanie S.
Marcy Hooper and the greatest treasure in the world /
Stephanie S. Tolan ; illustrations by Karen Milone.
p.   cm.
Summary: Third-grader Marcy, who can't seem to do anything right,
has an adventure involving a dragon and treasure, which bolsters her
self-esteem.
ISBN 0-688-10078-3
[1. Dragons—Fiction. 2. Self-respect—Fiction.] I. Milone-Dugan, Karen, ill. II. Title.
PZ7.T5735Mar   1991
[E]—dc20   91-12176   CIP   AC

To Zachary Craig Tolan,
the new generation
S.S.T.

Contents

Marcy Hooper
and the
Greatest Treasure
in the World

ONE

Another Bad Day

Marcy Hooper bit her eraser. The test was going badly. Did *puddle* have one *d* or two? She pulled at the carrot-colored curl that always fell into her eyes. If only she had studied her spelling words last night. At the front of the room, Mrs. Keller was already pronouncing the next word.

"Friend," Mrs. Keller said.

Marcy sighed and left *pud* next to number 8. She moved her pencil to number 9 and wrote an *f*. Then she wrote an *r*. So far, so good, she thought.

She added *end. Frend.* That looks wrong, she thought, and erased. She closed her eyes and tried to remember what the word looked like in her spelling book.

She couldn't. That was the trouble with words. She could never remember just how the letters were arranged. She loved to read, she really did. She only noticed what the words meant, though, not how they looked. Put together on a page, words made pictures in her mind. She could remember the pictures.

Marcy remembered exactly what the princess in her library book looked like. She remembered the fairy godmother, with her round face and short, shimmery wings. The fairy god-

mother seemed as real as Mrs. Keller. She could see the castle very clearly in her mind. It had turrets and banners waving in the wind. There was a moat with water that went all silver in the moonlight—

"Friend," Mrs. Keller said again.

Marcy jumped. There was no time to think about castles and moats. She looked at *frend* again. "You're just dumb," she whispered.

Gregory looked over at her. "What?" he asked quietly.

Marcy realized she'd said it out loud. She hadn't meant to. "Nothing," she answered fiercely.

"No talking, class," Mrs. Keller said, her voice firm. "This is a test." Marcy ducked her head and bit her eraser again. She talked to herself a lot. Sometimes she forgot and did it in school. *Freind,* she wrote. That looked better. A little better.

"And the last word for today," Mrs. Keller said, "balloon."

Ba-loon, Marcy sounded it in her head. She smiled. That's an easy one. She licked the tip of her pencil and wrote *baloon* next to number 10.

"Trade papers, please," Mrs. Keller said.

Marcy added *el* to *pud. Pudel.* Wrong, she thought. Gregory's paper landed on her desk. He held his hand out for hers. Quickly, she erased *pudel* and wrote *puddel.* There. She handed her paper to Gregory.

Ten minutes later, Marcy kicked the door open as she went out for recess. "Ouch!" she said. She had missed six whole words. Six! It was her worst spelling test ever. Only four right. Gregory had spelled all ten of them right. Gregory always got 100 on his spelling tests. She never did, not even when she studied. "Dumb, dumb, dumb!" she growled at herself.

"Did you say something?" Kate asked.

"No," Marcy answered.

"Come jump rope with us," Nicole called.

During recess yesterday, Marcy had tried to get the other girls to act out a story about a princess and a family of trolls and a magic unicorn. She had thought it would be much more fun than jumping rope. Kate and Nicole had said fairy tales were baby stuff. They laughed at her. So she had spent the whole recess sitting on the fence by herself. "Okay," she said now. Nobody ever laughed at people who jumped rope.

Marcy watched the other girls jump in under the twirling rope one at a time. They jumped on one foot, or turned in circles, or called for hot peppers and jumped so fast their feet became a blur. She could tell they were having fun. Maybe this time she could, too.

When it was Marcy's turn, she took a deep breath. The rope went around and around. She counted in her head—*one, two, three*—but she couldn't make herself jump in. She tried again, *one, two, three*—and flung herself under the rope. She jumped. The rope didn't stop twirling. "One," the turners called.

The rope was coming again. She jumped. "Two," the turners called. "Three . . . four . . . five." Marcy grinned. Jumping rope *was* fun! "Six . . . seven—"

The rope caught between her feet, and Marcy crashed to the ground. The rope lay like a dead snake underneath her. She looked up quickly. No one was actually laughing, but Kate was hiding a grin behind her hand.

"That's okay; you can start over," Nicole said.

"Thanks. Maybe tomorrow." Marcy stood up. She brushed the dirt off her bottom and walked carefully over to the school building. She leaned against the wall. She was the only girl in the third grade who couldn't jump rope, she

thought. Maybe the only one in the whole world.

Marcy thought about princesses. She thought about trolls and dragons, moats and castles. She wished she could be where there were castles instead of schools.

A fifth-grade boy flashed by on a skateboard. He leaned almost sideways as he swerved to miss the building. Marcy shuddered. Her brother, Sam, rode a skateboard like that. He rode a bike, too, with lots of gears. She couldn't even ride her two-wheeler. Her father had taken her training wheels off again last night. That's why she hadn't studied her spelling words. She had been trying to ride her bike. Her hands and knees hurt just thinking about it.

"It's only a matter of balance," her father had said. "Don't worry, you'll get it."

Marcy didn't think he was right. Maybe she

would never get it. She watched Kate and Nicole jumping hot peppers together. She wished she had her library book. Recess seemed unusually long today.

TWO

The Last Straw

It was Saturday morning—a bright, warm, red and gold October day. Marcy Hooper was in a hurry to go outside. She was going to spend the whole morning in her brother's tree house. She was going to take some crackers and a box of juice and her library book. It would be a whole morning with her favorite princess in a world of unicorns and fairy godmothers.

But she couldn't find her shoes. She went out into the hall in her sock feet. "Where are my shoes?" she yelled.

"You should wear them to bed," her brother, Sam, said. "That way you *couldn't* lose them." He hurried past her. He was wearing his Boy Scout uniform.

"Help me find them, please," Marcy said.

"No time. Ask Mom."

Mrs. Hooper sighed when Marcy asked. She was getting ready to go to the library, where she worked. She went to Marcy's room to look. She looked behind the wastebasket. She looked under the dirty clothes. She found them under the bed.

"But I looked there," Marcy said. "Twice."

Mrs. Hooper smiled. "Mothers are magic."

Marcy put on her shoes. Then she went into

the kitchen. Sam had finished his toast and was beginning on a big bowl of cereal.

"Could you boost me up into your tree house?" she asked.

Sam looked at his watch. "If you're ready before I have to go. I have to be at the church parking lot in fifteen minutes. Our troop's going to the Air Force Museum."

Marcy hurried. By the time Sam was finished with his cereal, Marcy had put a package of crackers and a juice box in a paper bag. She had gobbled down a piece of bread with peanut butter and had drunk half a glass of milk.

Mrs. Hooper came into the kitchen with a cup of coffee in her hand. "I'm late," she said. "Have fun, Sam." She kissed them both. "Your father's still asleep, Marcy. He worked late last night, so don't wake him except in an emergency. Okay?"

"Okay." Marcy knew what her mother meant

by an emergency. If she threw up, or started to bleed. That meant she couldn't try riding her bike. That's all right, she thought. I'm never going to go near that bike again.

Mrs. Hooper left. Sam drank the last of his orange juice and stood up. "Let's go," he said.

Marcy grabbed the bag with her crackers and juice. Then she remembered her book. "Just a minute. I have to get my library book."

"You and your fairy tales," Sam scoffed.

"I *like* fairy tales."

"But they aren't real." Sam put his Boy Scout cap on his head. "My troop leader says you should read books that prepare you for later life. Like how to become a pilot—or an astronaut."

"Mom says it's good to read, no matter what," Marcy said. Anyway, she wasn't sure she wanted to be prepared for later life, if it was like her life right now. "I'll be right back."

"I can't wait," Sam called as she ran down the hall to her room.

"It's okay. I know exactly where it is," Marcy said.

When she got back to the kitchen, Sam wasn't there. Outside, she saw him. He was halfway down the block already, pedaling his bike as fast as he could.

"No fair!" Marcy yelled after him. "You could have waited one lousy minute!" She kicked at the driveway. Then she went back into the house for her crackers and juice.

Outside again, she stood by the tree and looked up. The tree house was far above her head. She looked down and sighed. Her shadow stretched across the grass. "We'll just have to get up there by ourselves," she told it.

Nailed to the trunk of the tree was a narrow board. A foot above it was another. Sam had put them there, but he didn't use them any- more. He just grabbed a branch and swung up. Sam said anybody could climb the ladder steps. *Anybody*.

Marcy put down her book and her paper bag. She reached up to the first board. The tree house looked farther away than ever. "You'll never make it," she grumbled to herself. "You'll fall. You'll bleed and have to wake up Daddy."

There was nobody around to help her. And the day was too beautiful to spend reading indoors. Marcy held on to the first step. She took a deep breath. Then she put one foot on the tree trunk and pulled with both hands. Her foot slipped. She tried the other foot. She pulled. This time when her foot slipped, she bumped her chin on the board step. Hard. She rubbed her chin and squeezed her eyes shut so she wouldn't cry.

Marcy looked back at her house. Awful house, awful garage, awful yard. Then she looked at the street. Looking one way, she could see the tall buildings of downtown in the distance.

Looking the other way, she could see the

hills. They were far away, beyond the town and the houses. The sky above them was very blue. The hills were the colors of the autumn leaves, but soft with distance. Marcy sighed. They reminded her of the hills in her book, where the castle was with the flying pennants and the shining moat, where the princess lived.

The street stretched ahead as far as she could see. It looked as if it went all the way to the hills. "The castle," she whispered. "And the princess." Without another word, Marcy Hooper ran away.

THREE
The Country Road

Marcy Hooper walked four blocks. Then she stopped. "You aren't even any good at running away," she told herself. "You left the crackers and juice back there on the ground. The book, too!"

She pulled at the curl that was hanging in her

eyes. She hadn't really thought about what it meant to run away. Now she stood very still and thought about it. When you ran away, you were supposed to stay away for a long time. She had no food. She would get hungry.

When you ran away, you were supposed to stay overnight. In spite of the sun that was hot on her head, Marcy shivered. She didn't want to be away from home when it got dark. Even in her very own bedroom, she didn't like the dark. There were things in the dark. Shadows and shapes. And teeny little noises.

Marcy looked ahead at the hills against the blue sky. They didn't look as far away as before. The trees on their slopes looked brighter—red and orange and gold. She was four blocks closer to them now. She could imagine the gray stone castle and the pennants, flapping in the breeze. She could almost hear them.

"I'll go as far as the first hill and just look. It

will be an adventure. Then I'll come home."
She started walking again. "I'll be home for sup-
per. Maybe even for lunch."

Marcy walked and walked and walked. And
the sun got warmer and warmer. She didn't
recognize the houses anymore. She didn't know
the names of the streets. She had never been
so far from home by herself before.

The yards she passed got bigger and the
houses got smaller. The trees got closer together
and the houses got farther apart. Fewer and
fewer cars passed on the street, and they went
faster. First the sidewalk got narrow and full of
cracks. Then there was no sidewalk left at all.
She found herself on the gravel edge of a country
road.

Marcy stopped. Ahead, the road wound up
the first hill and disappeared into the trees. To
the right was a grassy field. It was dotted with
yellow and white flowers. On the left was a dusty
brown cornfield. The air all around was

loud with the whirring of insects.

"This is the country," Marcy said. "I walked all the way out to the country!" First she thought that was exciting. Then she thought it was dumb. She would have to walk all the way back. She was hot and thirsty and tired.

She looked at the hill. Now that she was up close, it didn't look so special anymore. "It's just a hill," she said. "No castle. No princess." Sam was right. Nothing she had come looking for was even real—not princesses, not unicorns, or trolls, or dragons, or fairy godmothers. The pictures in her mind were just that—pictures. "So there won't be an adventure," she told herself. "You might as well go home."

There was one tree not far away in the grassy field. Under that tree was a flat rock. "I'll just rest for a little while," Marcy said. "Then I'll go." She wished she'd brought the juice box at least.

Marcy waded through the tall grass. Grass-

hoppers whirred up in front of her. When she got to the rock, she sat down in the cool shade. She leaned back against the tree. The wind moved the grass in waves. She watched for a while. Then she closed her eyes.

"M-a-a-r-r-cy."

Marcy sat up. "What was that?"

"M-a-a-r-r-cy." It was a voice, a whispery, breezy voice. And she was sure it was calling her name.

Goose bumps rose on Marcy's arms. "Who's there?" She stood up and looked around. She saw only the rock, the tree, the grass. "Who's there?" she said again, louder this time.

FOUR

The Grass Nymph

I t's only the wind," Marcy told herself. "It's not a voice at all."

Just then, a slender figure no more than six inches tall swung out of a cluster of daisies. She landed lightly on the rock. The grass stem she had been swinging on snapped back. Marcy blinked and rubbed her eyes. The figure seemed to be a tiny woman, dressed in silvery green tights and tunic. Her long, straight hair was a deep forest green.

Marcy shook her head. "A giant grasshopper," she told herself firmly, and rubbed her eyes again. "Or a dragonfly." She bent to look more closely.

The figure drew herself up to her full height. She tossed her green hair and put her tiny hands on her hips. "Do I look like a dragonfly?" she asked. It was the whispery, breezy voice that had called Marcy's name.

Marcy closed her eyes very tightly. If she were imagining this, the woman would be gone when she opened them. Slowly, carefully, she peeked. The woman was still there. Was she asleep? Dreaming? Marcy pinched her leg. "Ouch!" The tiny woman smiled.

"Who are you?" Marcy asked finally. "*What* are you?"

"I am a grass nymph," the woman answered.

Now her voice sounded like water over stones. "And I bring you a message. You are right. There is no castle on that hill. There is no princess."

Marcy nodded. *And no grass nymph*, she wanted to add. "Ouch," she said. She had pinched herself harder this time. Still she was standing beside the rock. Still the sun shone on the nymph's green hair.

When the nymph spoke again, her voice sounded like dry leaves being scuffed underfoot. "You are also right that there will be no adventure. If that is how you want it. If you wish only to go home."

"I'm tired," Marcy said. "And thirsty."

"Then *do* go home. Adventures are seldom comfortable."

"Anyway, how could I have an adventure? You said there was no castle," Marcy reminded her. "No princess."

"The hill has many secrets. And many rewards."

"Rewards?" Marcy asked.

"Also many dangers."

"Rewards?" Marcy asked again. "What kinds of rewards?"

"Greater than any imagining." The nymph reached up and took hold of a grass stem that was leaning over the rock. "Do what you wish. But remember, Marcy. You must seek if you would find." With that, she gave a jump and swung gracefully out of sight among the daisies.

The rock was empty now. It was a flat gray shape with bits of something that glittered. An ant hurried across and down over the edge. Marcy rubbed her leg where it hurt. She looked at the hill. "Pooh," she said. "What kinds of rewards could be out here? Anyway, there's no such thing as a grass nymph. You imagined her. You're dreaming. You're nuts!" Then, very quietly, she murmured, "I wonder."

Marcy swallowed. She was very, very thirsty. "Time to go home," she told herself firmly. Isn't that what the nymph had said she should do? She glanced at the hill, bright in the sunlight.

Marcy pushed her way back through the grass to the road. When she got there, she looked toward town, toward her house. Then she turned and looked at the hill. "Rewards," she said.

"Dangers," she added.

Marcy Hooper stood for a long time, feeling the sun on her head. Then she began to walk. Dust swirled up around her feet. The road curved upward as she went. "I'll just go look," she whispered.

FIVE

Danger

Marcy walked up the road until she saw a path that led upward among the trees. She hesitated. It was narrow and steep and overgrown with weeds. The road, hot in the sunlight, was wide and well traveled. Marcy took the path.

She thought about rewards as she walked. What kinds of rewards could be out on this hill?

Greater than any imagining. She could imagine very well. She could imagine all kinds of great rewards. "Gold and silver," she said. "Jewels." She stopped. "Treasure," she whispered. "Buried treasure. The greatest treasure in the world!"

She began walking again, peering into the undergrowth as she went. Where could the treasure be? Under a rock? Beneath a giant tree? Inside a cave?

Treasure! If she had a treasure, she would be rich. And if she were rich, everything would be much easier.

She could buy so many shoes, she would always be able to find a pair. Her mother wouldn't have to find them for her. She could build a stairway up into the tree house. Her brother wouldn't have to boost her up. She could buy a battery-operated car. Her father could give her bike away to a poor child.

"If I paid him lots of money, maybe Gregory

would take my spelling tests," Marcy said. Being rich would be almost as good as having a fairy godmother, she thought.

Then she stopped. Her mouth fell open and her eyes got very wide. The path ended at a rocky ledge covered with moss. Above the ledge yawned a dark opening in the hill. The opening wasn't much larger than Marcy herself.

"A cave," she whispered.

She scrambled up onto the ledge and took a step into the cave. "Danger," she said, remembering. "The nymph said the hill had many dangers."

Marcy stood with one foot on the ledge and one foot inside the cave. Behind her was the light of the warm October day. Ahead was the cool darkness of the cave. *Darkness.* Marcy shivered.

"You must seek if you would find," she whispered. And she went inside.

The cave was like a big room with a high ceiling. Around her were rough stone walls. Beneath her was a rough stone floor. In the dim light from outside, she could see only walls and floor—no treasure.

Then Marcy noticed something darker in the wall in front of her. It was like a round shadow. She took a step forward. The shadow was a passageway. To the right, she saw another. To the left, another. The walls of the cave were full of dark openings leading deeper into the hillside. She thought for a moment. They had to lead somewhere. She tiptoed across the cave and peered into the one she had noticed first. It was dark—very dark—black.

"Oh, no," she said. "Not even for the greatest treasure in the world."

Marcy started to turn around and then stopped. "You must seek," she reminded herself. She took a deep breath and stepped into

the passageway. She stretched out her hands to feel her way. The walls were cool and a little bit damp. The air smelled old, somehow, and mossy. There was still some pale gray light. Soon the tunnel turned and the light was gone. Marcy stopped and put her hand in front of her face. She couldn't see it. She touched her nose and jumped. She had never seen darkness as dark as this.

"Treasure," she whispered. Feeling her way carefully, she went on. After a few more turns, she sensed space around her. She felt for the walls. There was one to her right but nothing to her left. "Treasure!" she shouted.

"Treasure, treasure, treasure," the echoes came back at her from all around.

"This is the dumbest thing you've ever done," she said.

"Done, done," the walls said.

Marcy turned to go back, but before she could

take a step, she heard a sound that froze her to the spot.

It was partly a gurgle and partly a growl. It grew louder. Then she heard a grating, scuffing sound as if someone were pushing something heavy over a rough floor. The sound came from the black emptiness behind her. "Enough adventure," Marcy said. "Time to go home."

She took two steps and felt the rock wall in front of her. She moved to the right. Wall. She moved to the left. Wall. Where was the passageway? The scuffing sound was growing louder, getting closer. It was joined by a thick puffing sound and a hot, smoky smell.

Marcy bit her lip to keep herself from screaming. She moved away from the sound, running her hands over the wall in front of her to find the edge of the passageway. Had she gotten herself turned around in the darkness? The gurgling growl came again, louder than ever.

She was sure the passageway had to be right here—

Suddenly, Marcy could see her hands and the stone wall in front of her. They were bathed in a dull reddish light. She turned, flattening her back against the hard stone. Into the light that now filled the cave came a dragon—a huge dragon.

It was exactly like the dragons she had seen in books. It had glittering scales and clawed feet and wings. Fire from its nostrils filled the cave with light and smoke.

Marcy stopped breathing. She felt her blood turning to ice under her skin. She opened her mouth to scream. Before the sound could come out, the dragon swooped down on her. It snatched her up in its front paws and carried her off down a damp, mossy tunnel.

SIX

Captured

Now Marcy screamed. Echoes bounced back at her. She kicked. She scratched. The dragon might as well have been made of iron for all the good that did. Its sharp scales bit into her waist. The smoke made her cough.

"The nymph said to go home," she told herself, and kicked again. "She said there was danger." Marcy bent over and bit the paw that held her. The scales hurt her teeth. She screamed again and again, until a coughing fit stopped her and the echoes quickly died away.

The dragon's fiery breath lit the tunnel. She could see that they were passing other tunnels that branched away on either side. The cave was like a maze. If she could ever get herself loose, how would she find her way out?

Marcy thought of her mother and her father and her brother. They didn't even know she was gone. When they found out, they wouldn't know where to look for her. There was no way they could save her. She wanted to cry.

Then she remembered Hansel and Gretel. They had found their way out of the dark forest. But she had no white stones to mark the way. She had no bread crumbs. She kicked at the dragon and her shoe skidded off its scales.

Shoes! She could drop her shoes as they went.

As the dragon clumped along, Marcy pried off one shoe and let it drop. She waited until the dragon had turned into a different tunnel, then she kicked off the other shoe. The dragon's paw tightened around her waist. She pounded on it with both fists. She wanted to bite again, but her teeth still hurt.

They made another turn. Marcy doubled over and scraped one sock down over her heel. She pushed it off and began working on the other sock. When that was gone, too, she tried to think of what she could drop next.

Before she could think of anything, they came out of the tunnel. The dragon's fire showed the high walls of a huge cavern. The cavern was so big, its edges were lost in shadow. It was so big, she couldn't see the top.

The dragon stopped at the edge of a deep, wide crack in the stone floor. In the flickering

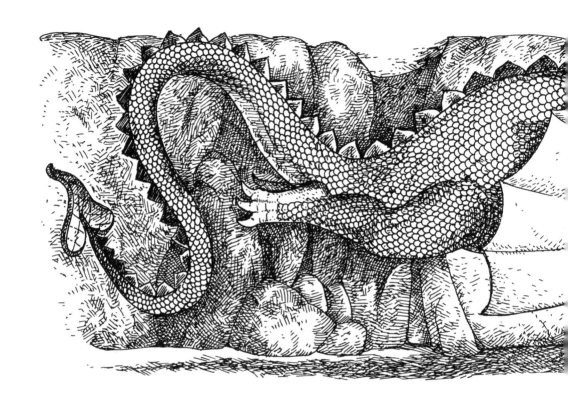

light, Marcy saw that the crack stretched across
the cavern. It disappeared into shadows on the
left. It disappeared into shadows on the right.
The dragon growled. It gurgled. Then, with

wings spread, it reared up on its back legs.

Marcy felt herself rising into the air. She clutched at the dragon's paw as the floor dropped away. The dragon's wings beat up and down, blowing smoke around her. Marcy coughed and choked and coughed again.

They were in the air now. The dragon was flying. Marcy closed her eyes. She didn't want to look. They were going up. And up. Then they tilted and started down. Suddenly, the paws around her waist let go. She was falling.

She screamed—and landed on the hard stone floor with a bump that jarred her teeth.

She opened her eyes. The dragon had flown over the crack and dropped her on the other side. Now it circled above her. The wind made by its wings stirred dirt on the floor. It billowed up around her. Marcy sneezed.

She looked at the crack in the floor. It was too wide to step across. It was too wide to jump across. And the tunnel that led out was on the other side of that crack. "You're trapped," Marcy told herself. "You're doomed."

"Doomed, doomed," the cavern walls repeated.

SEVEN

Treasure

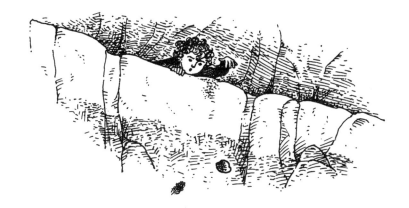

Marcy moved one leg. It worked. She moved the other leg. It worked, too. She stretched both arms over her head. "You're lucky," she said. "No broken bones." Her bottom hurt from landing on the stone floor, but otherwise she was okay. She stayed where she was and watched the dragon.

It circled above her and then flew back over the crack. Lighting its way with its fiery breath, the dragon landed on an enormous pile of sticks and twigs. It folded its wings and shuffled its huge feet. Then it turned around—once—twice—three times. With a snort and a gurgle, it lay down. It rested its head on its long, scaly tail and gurgled again. In a moment, the cave was filled with a sound like a buzz saw.

The dragon was asleep. With each rumbling snore, the cave went black. Then it was lit again with tiny flames that flickered from the dragon's nostrils when it breathed out. "I suppose it wants to rest before it eats," Marcy whispered. She shivered. She didn't want to be a dragon's after-nap snack. She had to escape.

Marcy waited until she was sure the dragon was sound asleep. Then she waited a minute more. Finally, she crawled to the edge of the crack and peered down. Even when the dragon's fire gave out its feeble light, the crack was black. It looked very deep. She found a bit of broken rock and dropped it over. There was no sound. "Deep," Marcy murmured. "Very deep!"

She began to crawl along the edge of the crack. Maybe it got narrower. Maybe it even ended. She might be able to go around it. In the gloomy light between the dragon's snores, she crawled quickly. In the darkness, she stayed still. The stone floor hurt her knees. She did her best to ignore the pain.

Once, just as the darkness came, she put her hand down on something big and hard and sharp. A stone. She picked it up and was about to throw it over the edge when the light came again. The stone seemed to catch fire. It shone with color—red and blue and green. Marcy caught her breath. This was no stone. It was a diamond. And it was bigger than her fist. "Treasure!" she whispered.

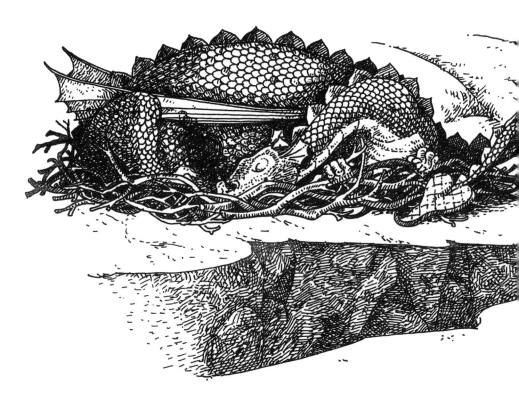

She looked around to see if there were any
others. There was nothing but the rough, dirty
stone floor. The diamond gleamed in her hand.
It wasn't a chest of jewels. It wasn't a
pile of gold. But it was enough—more than
enough.

The dragon snored and darkness fell. Marcy held the diamond carefully away from the edge of the crack. "It's all true," she said, her voice so low even she could hardly hear it. "A secret cave. And a great reward." She wanted to laugh. She wanted to shout. But she didn't.

She stuffed the diamond into the pocket of her jeans. It made an uncomfortable bulge. When the light came again, she crawled even faster. "Danger," she reminded herself in the blackness. "You still have to get out. You still have to get past the dragon."

Marcy crawled through the light of five noisy breaths. Then she came up against a wall of stone. She had found the end of the crack. It was still too wide to step across. It was still too wide to jump across. There was no way around. There was only the blank stone wall.

Marcy blinked and blinked to keep from crying. She sat down and dangled her bare feet over the edge of the crack. Sadly, she patted the bulge in her pocket. Treasure wasn't enough. Not even the greatest treasure in the world could help her in this cave.

"You could have been rich," she told herself. "Now all you'll be is dragon food."

A Way Out

The dragon gurgled and growled in its sleep. It twitched its great paws. "Nightmares," Marcy said. She hoped it wouldn't wake up grouchy— grouchy and hungry. She hoped it wouldn't wake up at all. The dragon snorted and its tail banged the floor. It exhaled a long, very bright flame.

In the flickering light, Marcy saw a ledge. It ran along the stone wall from her side of the crack to the dragon's side. It was about a foot below the floor of the cave.

She touched the ledge with one bare toe. It was rough and hard. It felt very solid. And it was wide enough for her whole foot—just barely wide enough. She scooted closer to the wall. She put her other foot on the ledge.

"Too narrow," she said. Very carefully, she stood up. She felt along the rock wall and found cracks to hold on to. A shiver went up her back when she thought about the darkness below her.

She slid one foot a little way along the ledge. She slid the other foot. "Too far across," she said as the dragon snored. She couldn't see to move her hands. She couldn't see to move her feet. "You'll never make it."

"Dragon food," she murmured.

When the light came again, she took a tiny

step. Then she took another. Inch by inch, she slid across the ledge. She balanced herself carefully, feeling for more handholds. In the darkness, she stood still. In the light, she moved. All the time, she felt the weight of the diamond in her pocket.

At last, Marcy saw that she was nearly across. Instead of waiting for the light, she took a step in the blackness. As her bare foot reached for solid rock, she found emptiness. Suddenly, she was sliding and bumping down the stone wall.

Her elbows scraped the rock and she tried to grab on to something. She wanted to scream, but she didn't. She bit her lip instead.

She landed on another ledge just as the light wavered on again above her. Blackness yawned beneath her. A long climb stretched above.

"Dumb, dumb, dumb!" Marcy said. "You were nearly there." She took a deep breath. She rubbed her scraped elbows. Then she began looking for handholds and footholds. "This time," she told herself sternly, "no hurrying."

Carefully, moving only in the light, she climbed. When she got back to the ledge, she pulled herself up over the edge of the crack. She was on the other side. She had made it. Only a few feet away, the dragon slept, snoring and growling. One ear twitched. Its tail jerked.

Marcy knew that once she left the cavern and the dragon's feeble light, she'd be lost. She wouldn't be able to find her socks and shoes. She wouldn't know which tunnels to choose. The dragon would surely wake up before she found her way out. She needed a light.

Slowly and quietly, Marcy tiptoed over to the dragon. Its eyelid fluttered, and she stopped. A curl of smoke and flame rose from its nostril and faded. Marcy held her breath through the darkness. Then she took hold of a branch that lay near the dragon's tail. She gave a tug, but the end of the branch was under the tail. She tugged harder.

The dragon rolled to one side a little. Its snore grew louder and then its flame leaped higher. Marcy waited, not moving. The dragon coughed a little, but it did not wake up. Quickly, she pulled the branch free. She tore off the small twigs. Then she crept toward the dragon's head. She held the branch as close to its nostril as she could. She tried not to breathe.

With the first snort, the end of the branch glowed red. With the second, it burst into flame. Marcy waited just long enough to be sure the flame was burning brightly. Then, with her torch held high, she ran for the dark opening the dragon had brought her through.

Inside the tunnel, her light fell on the first sock. She stuffed it into her pocket and hurried on. When the tunnel branched, she held her torch out into each passage. She found her second sock and went on.

Soon she'd found the first shoe. Marcy shoved her bare foot into it. In no time at all, she'd be outside. She'd be free with the treasure in her pocket!

Then she heard something that made her heart stand still. It was the dragon's gurgly growl, and the scraping sound. The dragon was awake. The sound wasn't behind her. It was off to the side.

"There must be another way out," she said, and nearly kicked herself. She hadn't thought of that. The dragon was looking for her. And it was getting closer.

Quickly, Marcy darted into the tunnel farthest from the sound. Her torchlight fell on her other shoe. She jammed it on and ran. She came to the wide place where the dragon had first caught her. There were three openings to choose from. Again she chose the one farthest from the dragon's growl. She followed the tunnel as it curved one way and another. Suddenly,

she could see a pale gray light ahead. It was the mouth of the cave. She was almost out!

She reached the end of her tunnel and peeked out. The cave was empty, its entrance bright with daylight. As she was about to run across it, a terrible roar filled her head. The dragon thundered out of one of the other passageways. It was in the cave now, between her and freedom. Long orange and blue flames were shooting from its nostrils in rage.

Marcy flung her torch behind her. It hit the stone floor and sputtered out. She pulled herself back into her tunnel and flattened herself against the wall. She could hear the sound of the dragon's flaming breath as it poked its head into the other passageways, one at a time. It would find her. She held her breath and listened. It had reached the tunnel next to the one where she was hiding. Hers would be next.

NINE

Freedom

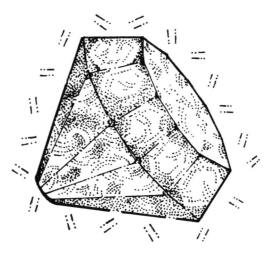

What could she do? She couldn't go back,
and she didn't dare run for the cave entrance.
The dragon would see her and sizzle her before
she was halfway there. Marcy felt the diamond
in her pocket pressing painfully against the rock
behind her. She pulled it out and held it up. It

glimmered faintly in the light from outside. "Treasure," she breathed. "Beautiful, beautiful treasure!" The dragon roared again, so loudly it seemed to shake the very rock she stood upon.

The flames from the dragon's nostrils licked the edges of her tunnel. "Now or never!" Marcy whispered. She pulled her arm back and threw the diamond as hard as she could. It struck the wall on the other side of the cave and clattered loudly to the floor.

When the dragon turned toward the noise, Marcy ran. Under its wing she went, and out onto the path beneath the trees.

The warmth and brightness of the afternoon struck her as she came out. She blinked and kept running down the path and out onto the road. She didn't stop until she reached the rock under the tree. There she flopped down to catch her breath. Her hair was stuck to her forehead. Her jeans were torn. Her elbows and knees ached. She was hotter and thirstier than ever, and very, very tired.

Insects buzzed around her. She waited for a small green woman to swing out of the grass. The nymph would say she'd warned her. The nymph would say she should have gone home. She had been dumb to go into the cave. But there was only a breeze, lightly stirring the grass.

With a miserable sigh, Marcy kicked off her shoes and put on her socks. She put her shoes back on and tied them carefully. "Just like you, Marcy Hooper, to throw away the treasure," she told herself.

Beneath the whir of insects, she heard again the whispery, breezy voice. "You have your treasure now . . . now . . . now."

Marcy peered into the grass. "No, I don't!" she said. "I threw it away. Back in that stupid cave. I threw it away!"

The breeze blew gently against her cheeks, but the voice did not come again. "Pooh," Marcy said, and stood up. She walked slowly back to the road and started home.

"You threw away the greatest treasure in the world!" she scolded herself as she went.

She took two more steps, then stopped. "But it worked," she said quietly. "It got me out of there."

"You could have been rich," she said, and walked on.

She stopped again. "I could have been dragon food."

"You're just dumb," she whispered. "Dumb, dumb, dumb." She took one step.

Then she stood still in the sun. "I thought of dropping my shoes and socks. I balanced myself on a narrow ledge. I climbed a rock wall. I made a torch. *I got out!*" Marcy shouted. She laughed. Then she shouted again, *"I got out!"*

She began walking. She walked faster and faster. Her knees hurt, but she barely noticed. Soon she came to the sidewalk. The houses got closer together. She began to recognize the names of the streets. Cars passed. Almost before she knew it, she had reached her backyard.

Never had her home looked so wonderful. She stood for a moment and stared at it. Great house, great garage, great yard. On the grass beside the tree was the paper bag. Next to it was her book. Marcy picked them up. "The juice will be too warm," she said.

She tucked the book into her jeans and held the bag in her teeth. Grabbing the first board step, she pulled herself up. She reached for the next step and climbed into the tree house. Marcy set her book down and took out her crackers and juice box. She sat with her feet dangling over the edge and took a sip of juice. It was warm. "That's okay," she said. "It's wet."

She ate some crackers and listened to the yellow leaves rustling over her head. She remembered the grass nymph's whispery voice. "You have your treasure now . . . now . . . now."

She looked down at her shadow on the ground. It seemed very far away. She smiled. "I climbed into the tree house all by myself," she said. "Me. Marcy Hooper."

Marcy leaned back against a large branch. She opened her book and began to read.